2.06

D0038647

A Note to Parents

Read to your child...

★ Reading aloud is one of the best ways to develop your child's love of reading. Read together at least 20 minutes each day.

★ Laughter is contagious! Read with feeling. Show your child that reading is fun.

★ Take time to answer questions your child may have about the story. Linger over pages that interest your child.

...and your child will read to you.

★ Follow cues from your child to know when he wants to join in the reading.

★ Support your young reader. Give him a word whenever he asks for it.

★ Praise your child as he progresses. Your encouraging words will build his confidence.

You can help your Level 1 reader.

★ Reading begins with knowing how a book works. Show your child the title and where the story begins.

★ Ask your child to find picture clues on each page. Talk about what is happening in the story.

★ Point to the words as you read so your child can make the connection between the print and the story.

★ Ask your child to point to words she knows.

★ Let your child supply the rhyming words.

Most of all, enjoy your reading time together!

—Bernice Cullinan, Ph.D.,
Professor of Reading, New York University

Reader's Digest Children's Books
Reader's Digest Road, Pleasantville, NY 10570-7000
Copyright © 1999 Reader's Digest Children's Publishing, Inc.
All rights reserved. Reader's Digest Children's Books and All-Star Readers are trademarks and Reader's Digest is a registered trademark of The Reader's Digest Association, Inc.
Fisher-Price trademarks are used under license from Fisher-Price, Inc., a subsidiary of Mattel, Inc., East Aurora, NY 14052.
Printed in Hong Kong.
10 9 8 7 6 5 4 3 2 1

Library of Congress Cataloging-in-Publication Data

Packard, Mary.
When I am big / by Mary Packard ; illustrated by Laura Rader.
p. cm. — (All-star readers. Level 1)
Summary: A boy enjoys imitating his big brother and dreams of the day when he will be big as well.
ISBN 1-57584-294-7 (pbk. : alk. paper)
[1. Growth—Fiction. 2. Brothers—Fiction. 3. Stories in rhyme.]
I. Rader, Laura, ill. II. Title. III. Series.
PZ8.3.P125Wh 1999 [E]—dc21 98-49565

When I Am Big

by Mary Packard
illustrated by Laura Rader

1
All-Star Readers™
Reader's Digest Children's Books™
Pleasantville, New York • Montréal, Québec

When I am big,
I will ride a big bike.

I will play lots of sports,

like my big brother, Mike.

When I am big,
I will run lots of races.

I will score lots of goals

and steal lots of bases.

When I am big,

I will be very strong.

I will skate on one leg

and play hard all day long.

When I am big,

I will be very quick.

I will run. I will pass.

I will block.

I will kick.

When I am big,

I will be VERY tall.

But for now I have Mike,

so I'm tall after all.

Color in the star next to each word you can read.

☆ a
☆ after
☆ all
☆ am
☆ and
☆ bases
☆ be
☆ big
☆ bike
☆ block
☆ brother
☆ but
☆ day
☆ for
☆ goals
☆ hard
☆ have
☆ I
☆ I'm
☆ kick
☆ leg
☆ like
☆ long
☆ lots
☆ Mike
☆ my
☆ now
☆ of
☆ on
☆ one
☆ pass
☆ play
☆ quick
☆ races
☆ ride
☆ run
☆ score
☆ skate
☆ so
☆ sports
☆ steal
☆ strong
☆ tall
☆ when
☆ will
☆ very